I Want to Be a Clown

Written by
Sharon Sliter Johnson

Illustrated by
Sandy Bradley

A little man was on a train.

The train came into town.

Where is the circus?

I want to be a clown.

I will wear this silly hat.

I will paint my nose bright red.

I will walk in these big shoes.

I will wear this yellow coat.

I will throw three blue balls.

I will tell a funny story.

I will make the children laugh.

I will ride this little bike.

There is the circus!

I want to be a clown!

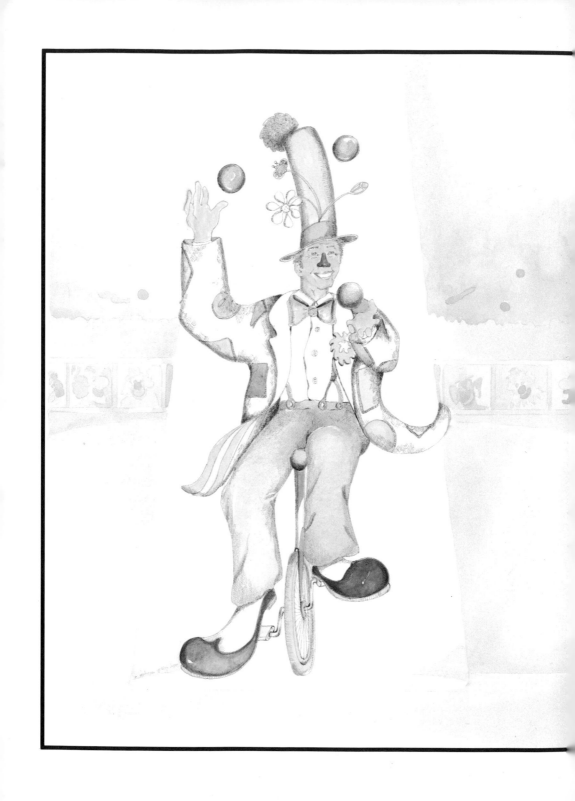